Magic Ballerina™

Delphie and the Masked Ball

Darcey Bussell

HarperCollins *Children's Books*

*To Phoebe and Zoe, as they are the inspiration
behind Magic Ballerina.*

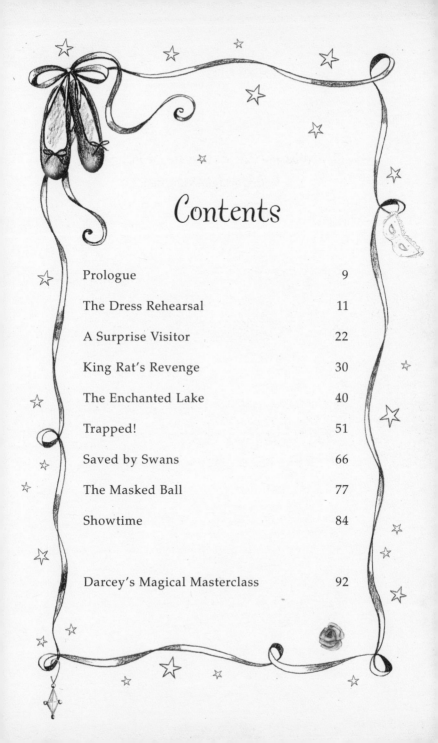

Contents

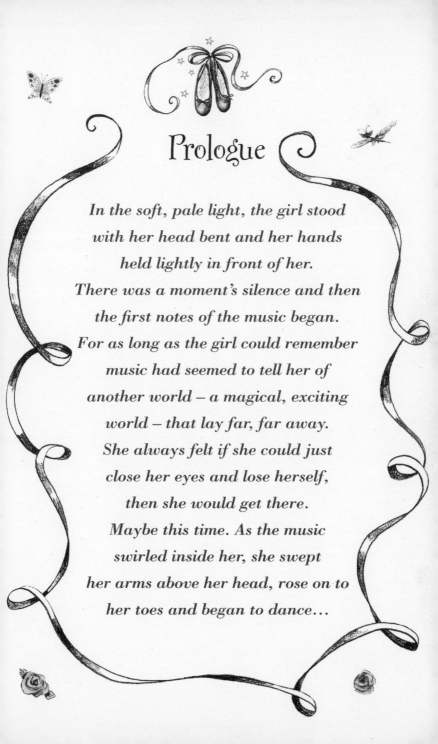

Prologue

*In the soft, pale light, the girl stood
with her head bent and her hands
held lightly in front of her.
There was a moment's silence and then
the first notes of the music began.
For as long as the girl could remember
music had seemed to tell her of
another world – a magical, exciting
world – that lay far, far away.
She always felt if she could just
close her eyes and lose herself,
then she would get there.
Maybe this time. As the music
swirled inside her, she swept
her arms above her head, rose on to
her toes and began to dance…*

The Dress Rehearsal

Delphie Durand danced in the bright
spotlight. Around her on stage, the other
girls from her ballet school stood in
darkness. Delphie was playing the main
part in the show – the Bluebird who
brought light back to the animals in the
woods. She finished with one leg stretched
out behind, her arms held out like wings,

holding the pose perfectly without a single wobble. Slowly the lights began to come up on the stage, as if sunlight was gently returning. The other dancers looked around in wonder and then suddenly they all began to dance...

Delphie skimmed across the floor with tiny steps. It was wonderful being up there and it reminded her of the times she had been in another theatre – a secret, magical one. For Delphie owned a pair of special red ballet shoes and when they started sparkling they whisked her away to a theatre in the magical land of Enchantia. All the characters from the different ballets lived in Enchantia and Delphie had enjoyed some great adventures there.

As the music ended and everyone
relaxed out of their final poses, Delphie
heard the sound of her ballet teacher,
Madame Za-Za, clapping from the hall.

"Well done, everyone," Madame Za-Za
called, smiling at them all. "That was a very
good dress rehearsal. Go and get changed

and then I will give you some notes so we can make the actual performance even better."

Delphie stretched. Her muscles felt warm and tingly. Her two friends, Lola and Poppy, came running over to her.

"You were brilliant, Delphie!" Lola exclaimed.

"I wasn't." Delphie blushed modestly. "I got some things wrong."

"I didn't see you get anything wrong at all," said Poppy loyally.

"Well, *I* did," came a voice behind them.

Delphie looked round. Sukie Taylor, one of the other girls in their dancing class, was standing behind them in her rabbit costume.

"Don't be so mean, Sukie!" Lola frowned.

"Ignore her," Poppy muttered to Delphie.
"She's just jealous."

Delphie had a feeling Poppy was right.
Sukie had been hoping she would be the
Bluebird and ever since Delphie had got
the part Sukie had been really horrid to her
in class.

Sukie scowled at Delphie. "Madame Za-Za should *never* have picked you to be the Bluebird. I'd have been much better!" And, tossing her head, she marched off.

Delphie felt the excitement and happiness fade away. But seeing Poppy looking cross, she forced herself to act like she didn't care. She wouldn't want her friends to be upset too. "Come on!" she said, trying to sound cheerful. "Let's go and get changed."

Delphie ran lightly off the stage with Poppy and Lola following. But as she reached the wings, someone came running towards her from the opposite direction. Delphie was taken by surprise and they collided heavily, with Delphie crashing to

16

the floor. Looking up, she realised it was Sukie.

"Ow!" Sukie said, rubbing her elbow. "Watch where you're going, Delphie!"

"You were the one who ran into me!" Delphie went to get up but pain stabbed through her left foot and she gasped. "Ow! My ankle!"

Poppy tried to help her, but when Delphie put her foot down it really hurt. "I can't stand," she said.

"I'll go and get Madame Za-Za!" Poppy dashed off.

Lola swung round to Sukie. "You did that on purpose!"

Sukie scowled. "What do you mean?"

"I bet you tripped Delphie up because you wanted her to be hurt!" Lola said accusingly. "You're her understudy so if she doesn't dance the part of the Bluebird, you will!"

Delphie stared. Was Lola right? Had Sukie really run into her on purpose?

Sukie turned red. "I... I didn't!" she stammered. "I..." She broke off as the backstage door opened and Madame Za-Za came hurrying into the wings. "Delphie! What's happened?"

18

Delphie blinked back the tears. "I've hurt my ankle."

"But how?" Madame Za-Za asked.

Sukie sent Delphie an imploring look. For a moment it was on the tip of Delphie's tongue to say that Sukie had run into her on purpose. But she didn't know that for sure and anyway she hated it when people told tales and got others into trouble. "I... I tripped," she said. "I was running off the stage and I just tripped over."

Poppy and Lola stared at her.

"That isn't what..." Lola began.

"It IS what happened," Delphie interrupted. She saw a look of relief flash across Sukie's face.

"Let me see." Madame Za-Za gently

19

unlaced Delphie's ballet shoe and turned
Delphie's ankle this way and that. Delphie
caught her breath. It really did hurt. "Can
you move your toes?" Madame Za-Za asked.

Delphie nodded and wriggled them.

"It is probably just a sprain," Madame
Za-Za said, after examining it a moment
longer. "But you'll need to go to hospital to

have it checked over. Hopefully it should
be back to normal in a week or so."

Poppy and Lola gasped.

"A week!" said Delphie in dismay. "But
what about the show?"

Madame Za-Za looked at her sadly. "I'm
afraid you're not going to be better in time
to dance in it, Delphie. Sukie will have to
take the part of the Bluebird."

Tears welled up in Delphie's eyes,
blinding her so she couldn't see the
expression on Sukie's face. She didn't need
to see it though. She knew just how
delighted Sukie would be!

A Surprise Visitor

The following day, Delphie lay on the sofa at home listening to the music of a ballet called *Swan Lake*, and rested her ankle. The doctor she had seen at the hospital had told her that it was indeed a nasty sprain and confirmed that she couldn't dance on it for at least a couple of weeks. Delphie's eyes were red with crying. She'd practised

so hard to be the Bluebird over the last
month and had been looking forward to
it so much. It was so unfair that Sukie
was getting to dance the part instead of
her.

The more Delphie thought about it, the
more she felt sure that Sukie had knocked
her over on purpose. It
was just the kind of thing
Sukie would do. Thinking
about it made fresh tears
spring to her eyes. She
blinked them away and tried to concentrate
on the music. She knew the piece well. It
was from a scene where the prince in the
story was standing near an enchanted lake
watching a group of swans dance for him,

23

led by the swan princess. Delphie sighed. She desperately wanted to be up practising and dancing, not lying on a sofa.

She looked at the floor. Her red ballet shoes were there. If only they would glow and take her to Enchantia. She had been willing them to do just that but nothing had happened yet. *Everything must be quiet in Enchantia*, thought Delphie. The shoes only took her to the magic land when the characters needed her help. Delphie didn't know whether to feel glad for her friends that everything must be OK or whether to wish something would go wrong so she could go and see them all!

She leaned over and picked the shoes up. The beautiful music from *Swan Lake* swelled

through the room. Delphie couldn't resist
slipping the ballet shoes on. She sighed
longingly. *If only I could get up and dance,*
she thought.

As she did up her ribbons, she heard the
front doorbell. Delphie's mum answered it.

There was the murmur of voices and then
Mrs Durand called from the hall, "Delphie!
There's a friend here from your ballet class
to see you... Sukie."

Sukie! What was she doing calling round?
Coming over to gloat probably, thought
Delphie, her heart sinking. The last thing
she felt like doing was seeing Sukie.

Then suddenly, amazingly enough, her
feet started to tingle. The ballet shoes were
sparkling and glowing!

The tingling feeling whooshed through
her body all the way from her toes to the
top of her head and the next minute she
was spinning up into the air and twirling
round in a rainbow of colours...

Delphie landed with a bump and looked

26

about, expecting to find herself in the
theatre again but this time she was standing
beside a window in a large round bedroom
that had a four-poster bed and a white
fluffy rug on the floor.

"Delphie!"

A beautiful girl with long brown hair
came hurrying over from the doorway,

her hands outstretched in greeting. She was wearing a long pale blue dress and a silver tiara. "Princess Aurelia!" Delphie gasped.

When she had last been to Enchantia, Delphie had managed to save Princess Aurelia from having to marry the evil King Rat.

Aurelia hugged her. "Oh, I'm so glad you've come, Delphie. I wished and wished the ballet shoes would bring you. I really need your help."

"Why? What's the matter?" Delphie asked the princess, pushing all thoughts of home to the back of her mind. "Is it King Rat again?"

"Yes. Oh, Delphie, look!" Aurelia pointed out of the window.

Delphie turned round. What she saw made her stare. The beautiful palace courtyard below was full of animals and birds – cats, dogs, horses, deer, goats and birds of all different colours. The air was filled with the sounds of squawking and whinnying, mewing and barking, bleating and hooting.

"What's happening? Why are there so many animals in the palace?" Delphie asked in astonishment.

"They aren't animals," Aurelia said miserably. "They're my parents' friends! King Rat has changed them all – perhaps forever!"

King Rat's Revenge

Aurelia started to explain to Delphie what
had happened. "It's all my fault," she
said, wringing her hands. "My parents are
away visiting far-off parts of the kingdom.
They're coming back this afternoon and
I thought it would be a really good idea if
I organised a surprise masked ball for
them. I secretly invited all their friends

and had beautiful animal and bird masks made for everyone to wear."

"That sounds lovely," said Delphie.

Aurelia nodded. "The trouble is I didn't invite King Rat."

"Well, of course you didn't," said Delphie, with a shudder. "He's horrible and he doesn't like dancing so he wouldn't want to go to a ball anyway."

"He might not like dancing but he loves eating!" said Aurelia. "He heard we were going to have a huge feast and a massive cake so when he realised that he hadn't been invited he was so cross that he cast a spell from his castle on all the masks. Everyone arrived this morning and as soon as they tried them on they

31

turned into animals and birds. My mother
and father are coming back in just a few
hours and I don't know what to do! Oh,
Delphie, please can you help me?"

Delphie wondered just how she could do
that. "Um… well…" She saw Aurelia's
desperate look. She couldn't let her down.
"I'll try," she promised. "Where's Sugar?"

she asked, thinking of the Sugar Plum Fairy. She and Delphie had become friends the first time Delphie had ever come to Enchantia and Sugar always had good ideas.

"She's gone to King Rat's castle," said Aurelia. "She heard a rumour that he might have made an antidote – a potion that will reverse the magic – in case any of *his* friends tried on one of the masks. If the rumour's true and we can get hold of the potion then we'll be able to turn everyone back into people again."

Just then there was a tinkle of beautiful music and a sweet smell of sugarplums filled the air. Suddenly the Sugar Plum Fairy was standing in front of them.

She was wearing a sparkling tutu and had
her long hair pulled back into a bun.
"Hello, Delphie!"

Gingerly, Delphie went to greet her but
as she stepped forward her foot didn't seem
to hurt any more. Delphie stopped for a
moment, puzzled. "It's better," she breathed.
"How can that be?"

"What's better? Are you OK, Delphie?" asked Sugar, seeing the look of surprise cross Delphie's face.

"Yes, I, I, well…" Delphie tailed off. *It has to be the magic of Enchantia*, she realised. Delighted that her ankle was feeling better, she ran over to Sugar. "Hello!" she said, hugging her.

"So did you get the antidote, Sugar?" Aurelia asked.

"Not exactly," Sugar said. "But I do know where it is."

"That's great," exclaimed Delphie. "Where? Is it in King Rat's castle?"

"No," said Sugar. "King Rat is still really cross with his guards since we managed to rescue the Nutcracker when you were first

here. He's decided the potion isn't safe
enough there so he's hidden it on Thorny
Island in the middle of the Enchanted Lake
just outside his castle."

"But that's no use!" cried Aurelia. "We'll
never be able to get it!" she finished,
beginning to cry.

Delphie looked thoughtful and was quiet for a moment. She knew that Sugar couldn't whisk them directly into King Rat's castle because his magic was too strong, but if this lake was outside of it, couldn't there be a chance?

"Can't you magic us there, Sugar?" Delphie asked. "Then we can just pick the potion up and come back?"

"I'd thought of that already," Sugar said, shaking her head. "The island and the lake are within King Rat's castle grounds, and so they are still under his spell. I can use my magic there, but it's very weak, and I can't take us to the island itself. The closest I could get us would be the woods just outside."

37

"Well, maybe that's OK," Delphie said thoughtfully. "We could sneak to the lake from there, find a boat and row over."

"I'm afraid that we can't do that," Sugar sighed. "The lake is enchanted, you see, no boat can cross it."

"Oh, what are we going to do?" wailed Aurelia. "My parents' friends are going to be animals forever!"

"Don't worry," Delphie said, going over and putting an arm around the princess's shoulders. She turned to Sugar. "Look, we're not going to get the potion back by staying around here. Why don't we go to the woods outside King Rat's castle anyway and see if we can think up something when we're there?"

"All right," agreed Sugar. She took hold
of Delphie's hands. Music filled the air and
lilac light started to dance around them.

"Good luck!" called Aurelia.

As Delphie felt herself starting to spin
round, she had a feeling they were going to
need it!

The Enchanted Lake

Delphie and Sugar landed near the edge of the thick wood. Through the trees Delphie could see the dark walls of King Rat's castle surrounded by a moat of muddy water. She shivered. There was the smell of rotting rubbish in the air.

"Where's the Enchanted Lake, Sugar?" She kept her voice low in case any of King

Rat's guards were nearby. They were all mice with sharp teeth who walked on their back legs and who were as tall as her. They were very scary!

"Just round to the left of the castle," Sugar whispered back. "Follow me!"

As they crept through the trees, Delphie tried to tread as lightly as possible. Every time a twig cracked under one of her feet she jumped and felt her skin prickle. But soon they had reached the edge of the woods. As Delphie gazed out through the trees she saw a dark lake.

"There it is," said Sugar.

The lake certainly looked very spooky. The water was as still as a mirror. In the centre of it was a small island covered with stunted, dying trees. Delphie could just see a grey stone tower, its turrets visible above the tops of the branches.

"We'll have to cross the grass to get to the lake," said Sugar. "Watch out for the mouse guards. Once we've left the woods I won't be able to magic us away from here if they see us." She checked around. "It looks like the coast is clear. Come on!"

But just as Sugar stepped out of the trees, Delphie heard the sound of marching. Suddenly a group of ten mice came patrolling round the castle walls. Delphie grabbed Sugar's arm, yanking her back into the woods, just in time.

Sugar caught her breath. The mice were wearing leather waistcoats and had long, sharp swords hanging from their belts. Their whiskers twitched and their eyes darted around suspiciously. Delphie and Sugar stood like statues. Delphie could feel her heart hammering in her chest. Would the mice see them – or maybe even smell them?

But to her relief, the mice marched on, disappearing from sight.

"That was close," Delphie whispered.

"Thanks for stopping me," breathed Sugar. "Hopefully if they've just been past, it means we've got a little while before they come back this way again."

She and Delphie stepped out from the trees, looked round cautiously and then ran as fast as they could across the grass towards the dark lake.

The water looked even more spooky close up. Delphie gulped. It was easy to imagine all sorts of horrible creatures lurking in its depths. She certainly didn't fancy trying to swim across it.

"So no boat can go through the water?" she questioned.

Sugar shook her head. "Any boat that tries will get thrown off."

Delphie thought hard. "Well, how about we don't use a boat, but use something like a raft instead? Maybe the enchantment only stops boats?"

Sugar looked doubtful.

"It's worth a try," said Delphie. "Can you magic one up?"

Sugar waved her wand. There was a

flash of light and suddenly there was a
wooden raft and two paddles on the grass
next to them. It looked a bit small and
unsteady, but Delphie guessed this was
because Sugar's magic was weaker within
King Rat's grounds.

Delphie started dragging the raft to the
lake. There was no time to lose!

The water rippled like oil as she pushed
the raft on to it. Delphie took a deep breath.
"Come on!" She crawled on top and it
bobbed up and down unsteadily beneath
her. Delphie felt fear catch in her throat as
she grabbed one of the paddles. Sugar
quickly joined her.

"Here goes!" said Delphie, trying not to
feel scared. She knelt up and pushed her

paddle against the bank. As the raft drifted out into the lake it started to swing round in a circle. Delphie put her paddle into the water and paddled hard against it but it had no effect. Sugar helped too but the raft continued to swing round in a circle. It started to spin faster and faster.

"It looks as though the enchantment *does* work on rafts as well as boats!" Sugar cried, dropping the paddle to grab on with both hands to stop herself from being swung into the dark water.

It was like being on the teacup ride at the fair but with no safety bar. The world blurred as they spun. Just when Delphie felt like she could hang on no longer, the raft suddenly shot backwards and hit the bank. Delphie and Sugar both somersaulted through the air and lay, sprawling, on the grass.

48

For a moment, Delphie just stayed there, her head spinning. She was very, very glad she hadn't landed in the water. She sat up and saw Sugar starting to sit up too. "That was horrible," said Delphie shakily.

"I guess we can't use a boat or a raft to get across the lake, then," said Sugar. "Just what *are* we going to do?"

Delphie looked out at the water. They couldn't sail across it, and there was no way she wanted to try swimming through it. "If only I had wings I could fly over the lake. Could you do that with your wings, Sugar?"

Sugar shook her head. "My flying doesn't work here either. But maybe... Of course!" she gasped. "That's it!"

"What?" asked Delphie.

Sugar smiled. "I can't fly there, but I've got some friends who might be able to help."

"Who?" demanded Delphie.

Sugar grinned. "The Swans, of course!"

Trapped!

Sugar waved her wand and music from *Swan Lake* filled the air. "We can summon the swans by dancing. We'll be using the magic of Enchantia, not my magic." she said. "Come on. Just copy me!"

The Sugar Plum Fairy ran forward with short steps, her toes outstretched and pointed. She jumped into the air, her left

arm moving forward and up, her eyes
following the line of her fingers as she held
one leg gracefully behind her. She landed in
perfect balance, ran on and jumped again.
Delphie wondered if her foot would be all
right, but as she stepped forward it was just
as it had been before and so she began to
copy Sugar, moving lightly on her toes and
keeping her arms as graceful as she could.

It felt good to be dancing again. Down and up. Down and Up. Her arms began to feel like wings and the joy of dancing filled her. This was so much fun. She could almost believe she was a real swan!

The music changed and Sugar started to spin round on the spot, balancing on one leg and swinging her other through the air, her arms moving out lightly to the side with every turn. It was a famous part of *Swan Lake* that Delphie had watched lots of times. Delphie tried to copy her. She could only manage two turns but Sugar kept on going, bending her knee and rising on to her toe each time.

Suddenly Delphie saw something that made her gasp. Twelve enormous white swans were flying across the sky towards them, their long necks outstretched. "Sugar! Look!" she cried.

Sugar ended her spin as the swans swept round them in a circle. For a moment all Delphie could see was a swirl of white feathers. The swans were about twice as large as normal swans. They landed and one of them stepped forward. She had beautiful dark eyes and held her head proudly.

"Sabrina!" Sugar greeted her warmly. "This is Delphie, the girl who has the magic ballet shoes."

Sabrina opened her beak as if she was smiling. "I've heard people talking about you," she said, "and about how you have been helping us. I'm pleased to finally meet you."

"And I... I'm pleased to meet you too," breathed Delphie, feeling slightly in awe of the beautiful, graceful swan in front of her. She curtsyed.

Sabrina looked pleased and the other swans nodded as if in approval.

"Why have you called us, Sugar?"
Sabrina looked uneasily at the castle. "We
don't like coming here. Last time we flew
over King Rat's castle, his guards attacked
us with bows and arrows. Two of us were
injured."

"That's awful!" exclaimed Delphie.

"Well, that's not going to happen this
time," Sugar said swiftly. "We don't need
you to stay here for long. We just really
need you to do us a quick favour. It's like
this…" She explained what King Rat had
been up to. "So do you think you could
possibly fly us to Thorny Island so that we
could fetch the potion?" she pleaded.

Sabrina touched her beak gently to
Sugar's shoulder. "Of course. I will be only

too glad to help you stop King Rat and his
evil plans." She looked at the swan behind
her. "Sahara. You and I will take Sugar and
Delphie on our backs."

The other swan nodded. "Climb on," she
said.

Sugar ran forward and lightly leapt on to
Sahara's back.

Delphie looked at
Sabrina who
nodded
encouragingly
and moved
closer. "Take hold
of the feathers
between my
wings, Delphie."

Delphie did as she was told, bent her knees and sprang as lightly as she could on to Sabrina's white back. She pulled her legs out of the way of the swan's wings and the two giant swans rose into the air, their great wings beating. Delphie hung on to Sabrina's feathers as they swooped over the lake. She didn't want to fall off into the water!

Sahara and Sabrina reached Thorny
Island and circled above the trees. "There's
the tower!" said Sugar.

The swans flew lower. The top of the

tower poked out from the trees. The swans flapped down and landed on its flat roof. There was a trap door in the centre with a metal ring in it.

"Come on!" said Sugar, jumping off Sahara's back. She tried to pull the trap door up. She heaved and pulled. "It's too heavy!" she panted.

Delphie and the swans hurried over to help. With all four of them pulling hard, they just about managed to get the trap door up. It crashed open on to the floor. Delphie peered down into the hole. There were stone steps inside leading downwards into darkness.

Delphie took a deep breath. The steps looked really spooky but if the potion was in the tower, there was only one thing for it. She started down them...

"Wait!" called Sugar. Pulling her wand out of her pocket she waved it high in the air. Sparkles of light streamed out and shot down the hole, lighting up the darkness with a silvery glow.

Delphie could see more clearly now, and she started to hurry down the steps. "Look!" she gasped, as the steps stopped in a round room, where a large black casket rested on a wooden table. Delphie ran down the rest of the steps with Sugar following and opened the lid of the casket.

Inside was a purple bottle.

Sugar touched the bottle with her wand. Sparks fizzed off it. "It's the magic potion!"

Delphie's heart leapt. She picked the
bottle up. "Now we just need to get it back
to the palace!"

Sahara and Sabrina flew them safely back
to the side of the lake where the other
swans were waiting.

"Thank you so much for flying us to
the tower!" Delphie said gratefully as
she got off Sabrina's back. "Now we'll
be able to use Sugar's magic to go back
to the palace and turn all of the King
and Queen's friends into people again!"

Sabrina smiled. "Good luck! I'm glad we
could help." She turned to the other swans.
"Come! Let us leave this place!"

They all rose into the air. "Goodbye, Delphie! Goodbye, Sugar!" they called.

"Goodbye!" Delphie and Sugar called back.

"We'd better get out of here too," Sugar said quickly to Delphie. "Let's go back to the woods and I'll magic us away before anyone sees us!"

But as they turned to run to the safety of the woods, Delphie saw something that made her freeze. A group of King Rat's guards were marching back round the castle walls in the other direction! "Look!" she cried.

"Oh no!" breathed Sugar as the guards suddenly saw them. The mice stared for a moment and then shouted, pulling their

swords out of their belts and
charging across the grass.

Delphie's heart
pounded. "What are
we going to do, Sugar?"

"Run for the woods!"
Sugar cried. "My magic
won't work properly until
we're there." They began to
race towards the trees but the mice realised
what they were doing and five of them
changed direction to cut them off.

"We're not going to be able to get there,
Sugar!" said Delphie, stopping. The mice
guards were closing in, their beady eyes
gleaming, their sharp swords waving.
"We're trapped!"

Saved by Swans

"You're our prisoners! We're going to take you to King Rat!" the mice shouted as they hurried towards Delphie and Sugar.

They were so close that Delphie could see their matted brown fur and yellow pointed teeth. She looked round desperately. There was no way of escape! They were going to

be captured and then what would King Rat
do to them?

"Delphie! Sugar!"

Hearing a voice in the sky, Delphie
looked up. "Sabrina!"

Sabrina and the other giant swans were
flying towards them, great wings beating
through the air.

"Climb up!" Sabrina cried, swooping
down beside Delphie.

Holding on tight to the potion with one
hand, Delphie scrambled on to Sabrina's
snow-white back. Looking over, she saw
Sugar leaping on to Sahara at the same
time. With three great thrusts of her wings
Sabrina took off into the sky again. Delphie
hung on tightly.

"Stop them!" she heard one of the guards shriek. "King Rat will go crazy if they escape!"

But it was too late. Sabrina and Sahara were already carrying Delphie and Sugar safely up into the sky. The other swans swooped down at the guards, beaks open.

"Argh!" the mice yelled, stumbling backwards as they tried to get away. But there was no escape. The swans dived towards them, knocking them down and sending them tumbling, nose over tail. Scrambling to their feet the mice ran back to the castle, shouting and yelling as the swans chased after them, nipping them with their sharp beaks.

Sabrina chuckled in delight as the mice threw themselves inside the castle and slammed the door firmly behind them. "Serves them right for shooting at us the other day!"

Delphie giggled and hugged her. Sabrina's feathers were so soft beneath her she felt like she was sitting on an enormous feather bed! "I'm so glad you came back."

"I heard shouting and saw what was happening," Sabrina said. "We'll take you all the way back to the palace. I'm good friends with Aurelia and the King and Queen. It would be wonderful to see them."

Delphie looked down. Beneath them she could see rolling green fields, with glittering streams winding through them.

There were sheep and lambs on the hillside, trees and cottages, a village with people in colourful clothes dancing in the village square, a town with tall houses, a house with an amazing garden surrounded by a high wall and a forest of dark trees. She laughed as the wind swept through her hair, whipping tears from her eyes. It was an amazing feeling to be swooping over Enchantia on the back of a giant swan!

Sabrina and the other swans could fly very fast and it wasn't long before Delphie saw the pointed turrets of the King and Queen's palace in the distance. "We're almost there!"

"Only just in time!" said Sugar from Sahara's back. "Look!" Beneath them, white horses were pulling a golden carriage along the road. "That's the King and Queen. They're only about twenty minutes away."

"Don't worry! We'll get there before them!" said Sabrina. She beat her wings faster and they raced towards the palace. Flying over the palace turrets, they swept down into the courtyard. It was still teeming with animals and birds and there was a chorus of surprised whinnies and

woofs and squawks as the swans landed.

Aurelia came rushing out of a door. "Sabrina! What are you doing here? Oh!" she gasped seeing Delphie.

"We're back!" Delphie cried, leaping off Sabrina's back. "And we've got the potion!"

Aurelia looked as if she couldn't believe it. "You've really got it?"

"Yes!" cried Delphie, holding the bottle up. "Sabrina and her friends helped us."

Sugar pirouetted. "Everything's going to be all right!"

"But we have to be quick," urged Delphie. "Your parents are coming along the road in their carriage. There isn't a minute to lose!"

"I'll get two more bottles to split the potion

and then we can all help," said Aurelia. She looked at Sabrina. "I can't wait to hear the full story!"

Aurelia raced off and came back with the two bottles. Sugar carefully split the purple liquid and they began. "Here goes!" she said, running lightly to a large horse who was watching nearby. She dripped a single drop on to his

back. There was a bright purple flash and the horse gave a whinny, which turned into

74

a happy shout. "I'm me again!" Where the horse had been standing there was now a tall, beaming man wearing a smart golden tunic and a horse mask.

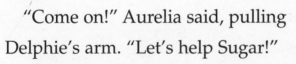

"Come on!" Aurelia said, pulling Delphie's arm. "Let's help Sugar!"

The three of them rushed around the courtyard as the animals and birds crowded round, eager to be turned back. At long last, the only creatures left were the twelve snow-white swans.

"We've done it!" Delphie exclaimed.

Just then, Griff, the guard who usually

stood at the palace gates, came hurrying into the courtyard. "Princess Aurelia! Your parents are on their way up to the palace!"

"Quick, everyone!" Aurelia cried. "Get ready for the ball!"

The Masked Ball

There was mad panic as everyone dashed about, talking about what had happened and trying to get themselves ready. Servants ran through the courtyard with big platters of food that they placed on long tables decorated with embroidered tablecloths, and an enormous white iced cake with seven tiers was wheeled through

to the centre of the courtyard. Drinks were
poured into silver goblets and musicians
assembled and started to play jaunty music
that seemed to catch at Delphie's toes,
making her want to run
and leap. Sugar danced
around the courtyard,
touching her wand to
every tree and
making sugarplums
grow on the branches,
filling the air with a
delicious sweet scent.

A trumpeter blew a fanfare and everyone
gathered into a smiling group with their
masks on. Sugar pirouetted up to Delphie
and touched her shoulder with her wand.

Delphie gasped as her clothes were changed into a beautiful red ball dress with a swirling skirt that was trimmed with feathers. She'd never worn anything so amazing. "Here!" said Sugar, magicking a swan mask and pressing it into her hands. As Delphie quickly put it on, the trumpeter blew another fanfare. Sabrina and her friends raised their wings, Griff threw open the door and the King and Queen's carriage swept through. The coachman reined in the horses.

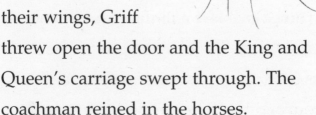

"What's all this?" the King boomed in astonishment as he and the Queen got out of the carriage.

Aurelia ran forward. "It's a surprise! I've organised a masked ball for you. All your friends are here!"

The Queen gazed round in delight. "But this is amazing! How did you manage it?"

Aurelia looked at Delphie and grinned. "With great difficulty. I'll tell you later, Mother, but Delphie and Sugar helped me."

"Thank you!" the Queen said, holding out her hand to Delphie. Delphie took it, sinking into a deep curtsey and bowing her head.

"I've got masks for you too," said Sugar, hurrying forward with a delicate cat mask for the Queen and a stag mask for the King.

The King put it on and beamed. "Let the ball begin!"

The musicians started playing again and suddenly the courtyard was filled with people dancing. Sugar grabbed Delphie's hands and they waltzed round and round together.

Delphie had never been to a ball before but it was exactly as she had imagined.

There was more food than anyone could
eat, delicious fruit punch to drink, clowns
and jesters, people juggling with fire and
lots and lots of dancing. At last, head
spinning, Delphie came to a stop beside
Sabrina who was sipping
water delicately out of a
golden bowl.

"Are you enjoying
yourself," Sabrina
asked with a
smile.

"Oh yes!"
breathed
Delphie. "Thank you so much for helping
us to get the potion back and making the
ball happen."

"It was my pleasure," the swan said. "I suppose you will be leaving us soon."

"I guess so," sighed Delphie, feeling her shoes begin to tingle.

"Well, maybe I will see you next time you come?" said Sabrina.

"I hope so," said Delphie, stroking the swan's soft neck. "I'll never forget flying on your back. It was amazing!"

"Delphie!" Sugar came over with Aurelia. "It's time to say goodbye."

"Goodbye!" Delphie sighed, giving them each a kiss on the cheek, before she was engulfed in a whirl of colours. In no time at all she was spinning round and round. The lights blurred and twinkled as she twisted and turned through the air…

Showtime

Delphie found herself back in her lounge, sitting on the sofa. She looked down. Her ball dress was gone…

Just at that moment, the door to the lounge opened and in came her mum with Sukie.

Suddenly everything came flooding back to Delphie. Of course, Sukie had called round before she left for Enchantia! Luckily,

as usual, although she had been in her magical world for hours, no time seemed to have passed here.

"Are you all right, Delphie?" Delphie's mum asked.

"Fine… I'm just fine," Delphie stuttered, realising she must be looking shocked and startled. "Er, hi, Sukie," she said, gathering herself back together. "What are you doing here?"

"Um, I just came to see you," Sukie said, looking awkward. She took a present wrapped in pink paper out of her bag. "I brought this for you."

"I'll go and get some drinks and biscuits," said Mrs Durand cheerfully as she went out.

Delphie stared at Sukie. Why was Sukie
giving her a present? For a moment she
wondered if it had something horrid in it
and was just a trick. "Thanks," she said
slowly. She undid the sellotape and found a
beautiful china ballerina wrapped in layers
of silver tissue paper inside. "It's beautiful,"
she said, unable to keep the surprise out of
her voice.

Sukie shifted uncomfortably from one foot to the other. "Oh, Delphie. I'm really sorry!" The words rushed out of her. "I didn't mean to run into you at the theatre. It really *was* an accident. I was just dashing back on stage because I'd left my rabbit ears there. I felt awful afterwards. I could tell you thought I had done it on purpose but you didn't say anything to Madame Za-Za and that was so nice of you. I'm really sorry you hurt your foot."

"My foot," Delphie breathed, suddenly remembering all the dancing she had been doing as she gazed down. Delicately she put her foot to the ground.

"I wish you could dance the part of the Bluebird still," Sukie was rushing on.

"How is your foot by the way?"

But Delphie wasn't really listening as she moved her toes. Her foot was fine. It was still fine! "Um, actually it's feeling much better!" Delphie grinned as her mum came in with the biscuits.

"Nice try, Delphie," her mum smiled. "But the doctor said it would be a couple of weeks before you can dance on it."

"I know, but look Mum!" Delphie jumped up and stood on her toes. She danced forward then stood on her foot, lifting her leg behind her just as she had to do as the Bluebird. "It really is fine!"

"Delphie! That's brilliant!" exclaimed Sukie, looking genuinely delighted. "You can be the Bluebird after all!"

Delphie pirouetted round the room,
clutching the china ballerina.

Mrs Durand stared. "That's a miracle!"

Delphie grinned and sprang into the air.
It wasn't a miracle – it was magic!

The next night, Delphie stood on the stage
holding hands with the other dancers,
curtseying as the audience applauded. She
knew she had performed better than she
ever had before. Her mum and dad were
sitting a few rows back, their faces glowing

with pride as they clapped. Glancing to her left, she saw Poppy and Lola grinning at her and Madame Za-Za standing just off-stage in the wings. As Delphie's eyes met her teacher's, Madame Za-Za gave a knowing smile and nodded encouragingly. Delphie stepped forward just as her teacher had told her to and swept into an extra deep curtsy. As the audience cheered, she felt like she was going to burst with happiness. Her life had changed so much since she had started doing ballet at Madame Za-Za's. She had danced the lead part in a show *and* had some amazing adventures in Enchantia. Whatever was going to happen next?

Darcey's Magical Masterclass

Sugar's Arabesque

The arabesque is a ballet pose that I'm
sure you've seen lots of times,
and it's one of Sugar's favourites!

1.
Start in first
position and
then gently
move your leg
backwards

2.
Begin to raise
your arms
until they are
around the
height of your
shoulders

3.
Lift your leg up from the ground, then sweep your arms out to the side

4.
Bring one arm forward to help with your balance and then hold the pose

Magic Ballerina™

Delphie and the Glass Slippers

King Rat has been playing around with the time in Enchantia, so even though Cinderella goes to the ball, she never gets to dance with the handsome Prince Charming! Can Delphie help her or will time run out for both of them?

Read on for a sneak preview of book four...

·°⭐·❊·⭐·°·❊·⭐·°

Delphie followed Cinderella into the carriage. The horses tossed their heads and set off at a smart canter. There were people hurrying through the streets. None of them looked very happy. *No wonder*, thought Delphie. *It must be awful to repeat the same day over and over again.*

Finally the coach stopped outside the Prince's palace. Delphie stared around in awe. Lights sparkled in the flowerbeds and great pots overflowed with sweet-scented roses. Music flooded out from the open doors. Guests in beautiful outfits were getting out of carriages but, just like the people in the streets, they didn't look very happy. Cinderella led the way to the entrance but as they reached the palace doors, a clock began to strike seven o'clock.

"Here we go again!" cried Cinders. Darkness fell and the whole world began to spin round. It got faster and faster and then suddenly stopped…

Darcey Bussell

Buy great books direct from HarperCollins
at **10%** off recommended retail price.
FREE postage and packing in the UK.

Delphie and the Magic Ballet Shoes	ISBN 978 000 728607 2
Delphie and the Magic Spell	ISBN 978 000 728608 9
Delphie and the Masked Ball	ISBN 978 000 728610 2
Delphie and the Glass Slippers	ISBN 978 000 728617 1
Delphie and the Fairy Godmother	ISBN 978 000 728611 9
Delphie and the Birthday Show	ISBN 978 000 728612 6

All priced at £3.99

To purchase by Visa/Mastercard/Switch simply call
08707871724 or fax on **08707871725**

To pay by cheque, send a copy of this form with a cheque made payable to
'HarperCollins Publishers' to: Mail Order Dept. (Ref: BOB4),
HarperCollins Publishers, Westerhill Road, Bishopbriggs, G64 2QT,
making sure to include your full name, postal address and phone number.

From time to time HarperCollins may wish to use your personal data
to send you details of other HarperCollins publications and offers.
If you wish to receive information on other HarperCollins publications
and offers please tick this box ☐

Do not send cash or currency. Prices correct at time of press.
Prices and availability are subject to change without notice.
Delivery overseas and to Ireland incurs a £2 per book postage and packing charge.